Rapunzel

Hilary Robinson and Martin Impey

W

FRANKLIN WATTS

Once upon a time, there lived a beautiful girl with long, golden hair. She was called Rapunzel, after the plants her mother loved to eat.

A wicked witch had stolen Rapunzel when she was a baby, and hidden her away at the top of a tower. The tower had one small window and no door.

Rapunzel was trapped. She could not escape. She was so bored that she sang songs all day long.

The witch visited the tower every day.
To get in, she would scream out:
"Rapunzel, Rapunzel, let down
your hair!"

Rapunzel, Rapunzel, let down your hair!

Then Rapunzel would let down her
long, golden hair. The witch would
climb up and get into the tower
through the small window.

One day, a prince rode by on his white horse. He could hear singing.

He looked up at the tower and could hear Rapunzel's beautiful voice. At once he fell in love with her.

The prince hid behind a tree and watched. He saw how the witch climbed up the wall and got into the tower.

Later, when the witch had gone,
the prince called: "Rapunzel Rapunzel,
let down your hair!"

The prince climbed into the tower.
He told Rapunzel that he wanted to
save her. As they talked, Rapunzel fell
in love with him. Over the next few
days, when the witch was away,
they planned her escape.

13

The prince brought her a bundle of
strong silk and Rapunzel spent many
hours making a ladder.

Before long she would be able to
climb out of the tower and be rescued
by the prince.

But when the witch next came to see
her, Rapunzel made a big mistake.
She forgot that the witch did not know
about the prince.

Rapunzel cried: "Why are you so much heavier than the prince? He can climb up my hair quickly."

The witch flew into a rage. She was so cross that she cut off Rapunzel's long hair.

"And to make sure he never ever finds you again I am going to hide you somewhere else," she screeched.

The witch left Rapunzel deep in the
dark wood. Then the witch went back
to the tower.

Later that day, the prince rode up
to the tower. He called:
"Rapunzel, Rapunzel, let down
your hair!"

Rapunzel, Rapunzel,
let down your hair!'

But, this time, when he climbed up
the tower he saw ...

… the angry witch!

"Away with you!" she cried. The prince fell into in the sharp brambles and thorns at the foot of the tower.

The prince's eyes were badly scratched
by the thorns. He could not see.

For two long years he wandered blindly,
lost in the woods.

Until, one day, he heard beautiful singing. "Is that Rapunzel?" he whispered. "Is that my beautiful Rapunzel?" he cried with happiness.

Rapunzel cradled the prince in her arms. Her tears of joy dripped on to his eyes. The prince found that he could see again!

The prince led Rapunzel away from the woods to his palace. The wicked witch was never seen again. They lived happily ever after.

About the story

Rapunzel is a German fairy tale. It featured in the collection of tales by the Brothers Grimm in 1812. The story of a maiden in a tower can be traced as far back as a story from Persia (modern Iran) written in the 10th century. In the Brothers Grimm version, Rapunzel's father is caught stealing a rapunzel plant for his pregnant wife from the witch's garden. He only escapes with his life by promising to give the witch his newborn child.

Be in the story!

Imagine you are Rapunzel when you have just given away the secret of the prince to the witch.

What will you
say to the witch
to convince her
not to punish you
or the prince?

Now imagine you are the witch.
What will you say to Rapunzel?

First published in 2014 by
Franklin Watts
338 Euston Road
London
NW1 3BH

Franklin Watts Australia
Level 17/207 Kent Street
Sydney
NSW 2000

A CIP catalogue record for this book is available
from the British Library.

The artwork for this story first appeared in
Leapfrog: Rapunzel

ISBN 978 1 4451 2859 7 (hbk)
ISBN 978 1 4451 2860 3 (pbk)
ISBN 978 1 4451 2862 7 (library ebook)
ISBN 978 1 4451 2861 0 (ebook)

Series Editor: Jackie Hamley
Series Advisor: Catherine Glavina
Series Designer: Cathryn Gilbert

Printed in China

Franklin Watts is a divison of
Hachette Children's Books,
an Hachette UK company.
www.hachette.co.uk